THE BOX BOYS

AND THE MAGIC SHELL

THE BOX BOYS
AND THE MAGIC SHELL

Jenny Nimmo

Illustrated by Anthony Lewis

Hodder
Children's
Books

a division of Hodder Headline plc

Published in Great Britain in 1999 by
Hodder Children's Books

10 9 8 7 6 5 4 3 2 1

A Catalogue record for this book is available from the British
Library

ISBN 0 340 73290 3

Printed and bound in Great Britain by Guernsey Press,
Guernsey, Channel Islands

Hodder Children's Books
a division of Hodder Headline plc
338 Euston Road
London NW1 3BH

For the children and staff of
Buttington County Primary School

Chapter One

"John! John! Help me!"

John Box opened one eye. It was still dark. Who was calling him? he didn't want to get out of bed. He didn't even want to wake up. It was much too early.

"Please, help me."
Such a tiny, faraway voice,
and yet it seemed to be right
inside his ear.
"Please, help me"
"Who are you?" John
whispered.

But the voice wouldn't tell.

"*Take me back! Take me back!*"

There was a splash and a rustle, like water on pebbles.

"*Pleeassh!*"

Now John was wide awake. What could it be, splashing and rustling inside his ear. He jumped out of bed and began to look around his room.

Under the bed, behind the cupboard, in all the drawers. Nothing. But the voice was still calling,

"Whish! Whish! Ssshhh!"
"Take me back!"

John tiptoed downstairs.
"Pleeeash!"
He didn't want to wake his mum and dad, they'd think he'd heard burglars. And somehow John knew it wasn't burglars.

The little voice was closer now. It seemed to be coming from under the stairs. John opened the cupboard door, and there, at his feet, was the shell that Uncle Vince had given him.

Uncle Vince was a great traveller and he'd brought the giant conch shell all the way from the West Indies.

"Mum must have put it in the cupboard," John murmured. He picked up the shell.

Dawn was beginning to creep through the windows and in the pale light the shell looked beautiful.

It glowed like a pearl.

John took it into the kitchen.
His dog, Bunk, was fast alseep
in his basket, but when John
came in he lifted his head.

"Ssh" said John. "Don't
bark!" Bunk gave a little whine
and went back to sleep.

The sound of the sea was very close now. It was like standing on a beach with the tide rolling in.

Wish Wish
Sshh Sshh
John put the shell to his ear.

"Take me back to the sea . . . the sea . . . the sea . . ." rustled the voice.

"I can't." said John." I don't live near the sea."

"Please," begged the shell.

"All right, I'll try," said John. "But I don't know how. I'll have to sleep on it." He carried

the shell up to his room and
put it on the windowsill, where
it rustled and swished and
whispered until the sun came
up. And then it fell silent.
Perhaps it was sleeping.

John closed his eyes. Thank
goodness," he said, and he too
fell asleep.

So he didn't see the shell
rocking gently on the window
sill. Rock, rock, rock – as
though it were at sea.

Chapter Two

"Wake up, John!" His mother popped her head around the door. "You can't sleep all day, just because it's Saturday."

John sat up. "The shell woke

me up," he said sleepily. "It kept me awake for ages, so now I'm tired."

"The shell?" His mum came into the room.

"The conch shell that Uncle Vince brought," said John. "It was swishing and whispering like something alive." His mum picked up the shell and held it to her ear. "I can't hear anything," she said.

"It's fallen asleep," John told her. "Even shells must get tired."

"Oh, John." His mum smiled. "You've been dreaming."

"I haven't."

"Scott's downstairs," she said. "He's brought his bike round."

"Great!" John jumped out of bed, scrambled into his clothes and ran downstairs.

Scott was eating toast in the kitchen. "Shall we go to the park," he said eagerly.

John hesitated. "There's something I want to show you first."

"What's that?"

John told him about the conch shell.

"You mean it really talks?"
Scott looked amazed.

"It was quiet when Mum
picked it up," John said. "But
perhaps it'll talk to you."

"Let's go and see."

"Not till John's had his
breakfast," said his mother,
coming into the kitchen.

As soon as John had eaten his boiled egg, the Box Boys rushed upstairs, taking two steps at a time.

"Wow!" said Scott, when he saw the shell. "It's fantastic." He put the shell to his ear.

"Can't hear anything, though."

"Maybe it's still asleep," said John. "Let's give it a rest and come back later."

They took their bikes into the park and whizzed around the lake seven times.

Then they sat by the water
for a while, and watched a
duck and her seven ducklings,
until John said, "I can't wait
any longer. I want you to hear
that shell."

When they got back to John's
house, they found that
something had happened in
John's room.

The shell had fallen on the floor.

"That's funny," Scott picked it up. "I'm sure I put it where it wouldn't fall."

"Help!" said the shell, and four big drops of water spilled out, splashing Scott's hand. It was almost as if it were crying.

Scott was so surprised he nearly dropped the shell. "I heard it," he cried. "It spoke!"

"I told you," said John.

"Take me back!" hissed the shell,
John took the shell from Scott and spoke into the shining whorls that curled up inside it, like an ear. "We can't, not yet," he whispered, "the sea's too far away."

"Wait a minute," Scott said. "We could go to the sea. We could go tomorrow."

"How?" asked John. "Dad has to work on Sunday and he always takes the car."

"My dad goes fishing," Scott said, "but Mum doesn't. She can drive."

"But could she . . . would she take us to the seaside?" asked John.

"I'll promise to clean the car," said Scott, "and tidy my room, and work harder at school. That should do it. She'll have to say yes."

"Yes! Yes! Yes!" cried John

bouncing on to his bed.

"Hurry!" whispered the shell.

John stopped bouncing. The journey to the sea was very urgent.

The shell grew cold. The sound of waves echoed inside it. *Splash! Splash! Splash!*

"How did this happen to you?" Scott asked the shell. "When did you find your voice?"

" I remembered my home in the water, the warm, warm water under the sun. I know I'm only a shell. The mollusc inside me was eaten long ago, but I still remember . . . remember . . . remember. I remember the pearl they took from me. A shiny pink pearl as big as your fingertip."

"We'll get you back," Scott promised. "Tomorrow. Can you just wait one more night?"

"I'll try," said the shell in a very faint voice.

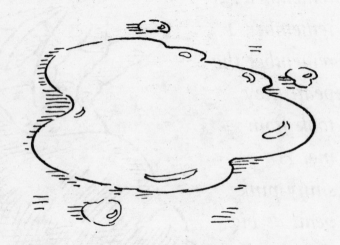

Chapter Three

The shell didn't speak again that
day. It seemed to have used up
all its strength. But in the night
it began to rock again, and the
sound of the sea swished and

rustled inside it.

John could hardly sleep a wink. He kept wondering if Scott's mum would take them to the sea: Scott and himself and the shell.

He needn't have worried. Early next morning Scott was ringing the doorbell, then leaping in to tell John the good news.

"It's on," cried Scott. "Mum says to bring sandwiches and something to drink. We can be there in two hours."

"What's going on?" asked John's mum. "Where are you going?"

"To the sea," John told her. "Scott's mum is taking us, and we're going to throw the conch shell back into the sea."

"You can't do that." John's mum looked cross. "It's a beautiful shell, and a present from Uncle Vince."

"But it's my shell now," said John, "and it wants to go back to the sea. It told me."

"It's true, Mrs Box," said Scott.

"You're both being silly," she said.

"It did! It did!" cried John. He rushed upstairs and brought the conch shell down to the kitchen. "Listen to it," he said, putting the shell into his mum's hands.

She lifted the
shell to her ear.
"I don't hear
any …" she
began, and then
her eyes opened
very wide.

"*Whish . . . whish . . .*" came
the echoey voice of the shell.
"*Pleeeash . . . pleeash . . . please!*"
John's mother handed the
shell back to John. "Perhaps I
was wrong," she said. "I'll make
you some sandwiches."

As his mum buttered the bread
and grated the cheese, John
wondered whether she wanted
to come with them. She could

do with a day by the sea, he thought.

It was almost as if someone heard John thinking, because the next thing he knew, Scott's mother was in the kitchen asking John's mum to come with them.

"To keep me company," she said. "The boys will want to go off on their own, and I'll be stuck with no one to talk to. I don't know what this is all about, but it suddenly seems a lovely idea to go the sea. It's going to be hot today."

"Well thank you," said John's mum. "I'd love to come."

Bunk started to bark and John said "What about Bunk? We can't leave him behind."

"Bunk can come with us, can't he, Mum?" said Scott.

"Of course he can. The more the merrier," she said.

When the food was packed and the towels stacked in the boot, everyone piled into Scott's parents' long green car.

Bunk squeezed between the
boys and John held the conch
shell very tight. He could feel it
humming under his fingers.

It made no sound but he knew
it was happy.
"Just feel it,"
he said,
passing the
shell to
Scott.

Scott took
the shell.

"It's like a
cat's purr," he
murmured.
"But I
still don't
understand
how the shell
came alive."

41

Almost before they knew it they'd reached the sea. As soon as the car was parked, the boys slid out and ran towards the dunes with Bunk barking at their heels.

Their mothers followed,
laughing together.

The tide was out and the
beach was dotted with children
and dogs and people strolling
over the sand.

John and Scott, already in
swimming trunks, pulled off
their jeans and raced towards
the sea. It looked so far away.

They didn't notice the group of boys, playing round a stretch of rocks. The boys were older than John and Scott and one of them was a tall, red-haired boy. The Box Boys had seen him before – once when the fair came to town. They remembered his name was Pete.

"What have you got there?" Pete shouted.

But the Box Boys kept on running, while Pete chased after them. "Answer me!" he yelled.

He had very long legs and in a
few seconds, he'd reached John
and pulled the conch out of his
hands.

"No!" cried the Box Boys
and Bunk gave an angry bark.

"Ha Ha!" laughed Pete. "You
can't catch me," and he jumped
on to the rocks and leapt away.

Chapter Four

"Come back!" John screamed.
"Give me my shell!"
  Scott rushed after the boy.
"It's no good," he shouted.
"We'll have to force him to

give it back, somehow."

John followed Scott on to the rocks. Pete was wearing trainers but John and Scott had left their shoes on the beach. The limpets and mussels that covered the rocks pricked their bare feet like tiny daggers.

"Ouch! Ooh! Ow!" yelled the Box Boys.

Bunk darted round the rocks, growling helplessly.

He didn't
like the
look of
the
spiky
limpets.

John began
to walk on all fours. His hands
didn't seem as soft as his feet.

"It's no good," he moaned.
"We'll never catch up with
him."

"We will! We will!" cried
Scott.

But the red-haired boy was
far ahead. And then, suddenly,
the conch shell
made an
extraordinary
noise. The sort of
sound that comes
from a giant horn
in an orchestra.

Pete stared at the
shell in horror,
and then he
dropped it.

The shell
headed for
the rocks,
while the
boys just
gazed at in
disbelief.

Pete's gang raced round the
rocks to see what had happened.

"What's up, Pete?" they cried.
"What's the matter?"

"It honked," said Pete. "The shell honked."

"Come off it, Pete," called one of his friends. "That was you. Shells don't honk by themselves." And they all began to laugh.

John and Scott limped up to the shell. A long crack ran from the curled opening almost to its pointed tip.

"What have you done?" John
glared at Pete.

Pete looked a bit scared.
"N . . . nothing," he said.
"You can keep your mouldy old
shell. I reckon its haunted." And
he hared off across the rocks as
fast as he could.

"Help me!" murmured the shell.

"What can we do to help you?" asked Scott.

"Take me to the seeeeaaaa," whispered the shell.

Very carefully, and with both hands, John lifted the shell off the rocks.

He was afraid it might break
apart, but luckily the crack
wasn't quite long enough.

Scott jumped off the rocks
and John handed the shell
down to him.

Then John stepped on to the sand. Together the Box Boys walked towards the sea. As they got closer to the water the shell began to rustle and gurgle and hum.

"I'm going home, home, home," it sang.

They had reached the edge of the surf. The water tickled their toes and soothed their stinging feet.

Bunk splashed joyfully beside them.

"*Deeper,*" sighed the shell. "*You'll have to go deeper.*"
The Box Boys stepped into the sea. Soon the water was up to their knees.
Their mums had walked across the sand behind them.

"Don't go out too far," called Scott's mum, dipping her toes in the water.

"We won't," said Scott.

"*Deeper*," whispered the shell.

Now the Box Boys had to wade. The water was up to their waists. They noticed that no one else was out as far as they were. Bunk had started to swim.

"*Deeper*," urged the shell, whose voice had grown deeper.

John heard his mother's voice. "No further John!"

He turned and saw her standing at the edge of the water, waving.

"*Deeper*," begged the shell.

"No," said John. "We must go back."

"One more step," said Scott.

They took one more step, then Scott held his arms out before him.

His hands lay in the water, with the shell resting on his palms.

As he moved his palms apart,
the shell floated free and
bobbed away from them.

"*Thank you!*" the shell
seemed to boom. It's voice had
become stronger and musical.

The sound echoed across the
sea and made the water tingle.
Every ripple seemed to be
tipped with shining colours –
red, green and gold.

"We saved it," said John.
Before the sea could pull them
off their feet, the Box Boys
turned and plunged towards the
beach. Bunk got there first.

"Did you hear it?" Scott
called to his mum. "Did you
hear the shell?"

His mum just grinned and
waved, but when the boys were
on dry land again, she said, "I
did hear something. It was like
a foghorn."

"No, it was more musical," said John's mum. "More like the horn in an orchestra."

"All right," laughed Scott's mum, "a musical horn. Now, let's get these boys dry. They're shivering."

When the boys were dry and munching sandwiches, John's mum said, "Whatever it was that made us decide come to the sea today, I'm very glad we did. I wouldn't have missed it for anything."

The Box Boys looked at each other and then out to sea. "It was the magic shell," they said, and smiled.